This book belongs to

ices
ings

For Eleanor Fegan, with love – SR
"Hello Florence!" – CT

LONDON, NEW YORK, SYDNEY, DELHI, PARIS
MUNICH and JOHANNESBURG

First published in Great Britain in 2001
by Dorling Kindersley Limited,
80 Strand, London WC2R ORL

2 4 6 8 10 9 7 5 3 1

Text copyright © 2001 Shen Roddie
Illustrations copyright © 2001 Carol Thompson
The author's and illustrator's moral rights have been asserted.

A CIP catalogue record for this book is available from the British Library.

ISBN 0-7513-7252-8

Colour reproduction by Dot Gradations, UK
Printed in China by South China Press

See our complete
catalogue at
www.dk.com

Goodbye, Hello!

Shen Roddie

Illustrated by Carol Thompson

A Pearson Company

Goodbye, moon!

Hello, sun!

I wonder what I'll do today?

Goodbye, nappy

Hello, potty!

Listen to the ting-a-ling!

Goodbye,
high chair!

Hello, low chair!

I spy bananas for breakfast.

Goodbye, bottle!